SIMPSON'S SHEEP WON'T GO TO SLEEP!

Bruce Arant

PETER PAUPER PRESS, INC.
White Plains, New York

To Norah, Pippa, and all my other little lambs, who are yet to be

Thanks to my agent, Marie Galastro of MLG & Associates,
for her guidance and expertise

Library of Congress Cataloging-in-Publication Data

Arant, Bruce, author, illustrator.
  Simpson's sheep won't go to sleep! / by Bruce Arant. -- First edition.
      pages cm
  Summary: "When Farmer Simpson tries to put his sheep to bed, they think of every excuse to stay
awake. Finally, he thinks of a warm and cozy solution that will help lull the sheep right to sleep"--
Provided by publisher.
  ISBN 978-1-4413-1359-1 (hardcover : alk. paper) [1. Stories in rhyme. 2. Bedtime--Fiction.
3. Sleep--Fiction. 4. Sheep--Fiction.] I. Title. II. Title: Simpson's sheep will not go to sleep!
  PZ8.3.A576Si 2013
  [E]--dc23
                                              2013010074

Published by Peter Pauper Press, Inc.
202 Mamaroneck Avenue
White Plains, New York 10601

Published in the United Kingdom and Europe by Peter Pauper Press, Inc.
c/o White Pebble International
Unit 2, Plot 11 Terminus Rd.
Chichester, West Sussex PO19 8TX, UK

Designed by Heather Zschock

ISBN 978-1-4413-1359-1
Manufactured for Peter Pauper Press, Inc.
Printed in China

7 6 5 4 3 2 1

Visit us at www.peterpauper.com

SIMPSON'S SHEEP
WON'T GO TO SLEEP!

Farmer Simpson works all day.
He plants his corn and beans and hay.

His feet get tired, his nose gets red.
At night, he likes to go to bed.

His pigs and cows all cuddle tight.
With grunts and snorts, they sleep all night.

His ducks and hens lie in a heap,
then quack and cluck themselves to sleep.

Each night before he gets *his* rest,
the farmer tries his very best
to gather up his flock of sheep
and tell them that it's time to sleep.

But they all have excuses why
they can't lie down, or even try.

They need a drink. They want a snack.
They have to "go"! They like to yack.
The ground's too hard. The grass is wet.
They'll settle down . . . but not quite yet.

The sky's too dark. The moon's too bright.
Then someone starts a tickle fight.
They smell a smell. They have an itch.
They can't lie still, they have to twitch.

They think of every reason why
to stay awake beneath the sky.
It sometimes makes poor Simpson weep.
This time of night, he needs his sleep!

After weeks of little rest,
the tired farmer felt distressed.
And then to make him feel more rotten,
he recalled what he'd forgotten.

Up to his knees in
fluffy fleece,
he thought of his
dear wife, Bernice.

"Her birthday's here—today's the date!
What should I do to celebrate?"

So Simpson sat and thought a while,
and wondered how to make her smile.
"I'll buy a present, soft and pretty,
from the best store in the city."

Farmer Simpson went to town
to buy his wife a sleeping gown.

And as he chose which gown to buy,
Some *other* presents caught his eye.
"I'll buy these for my sheep," he said,
"to give them when it's time for bed."

That night at bedtime—8 o'clock,
he gently covered up his flock
with cozy blankets, soft and snug,
as comfy as a mother's hug.

Then Farmer Simpson watched his sheep.
Their eyes drooped low. Their "baaah's," baaah'ed deep.
In blankets warm, they couldn't make
one poor excuse to stay awake.

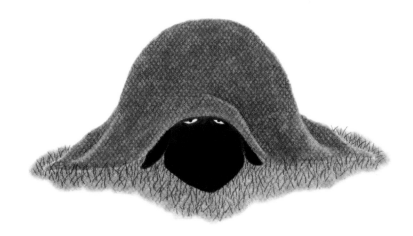

And one by one, that farmer knew,
each cuddly lamb, and ram, and ewe,
would curl up cozy on the ground
and wouldn't even make a sound.

Well . . . just one sound, but nothing more.
They made a sleepy, sheepy snore…

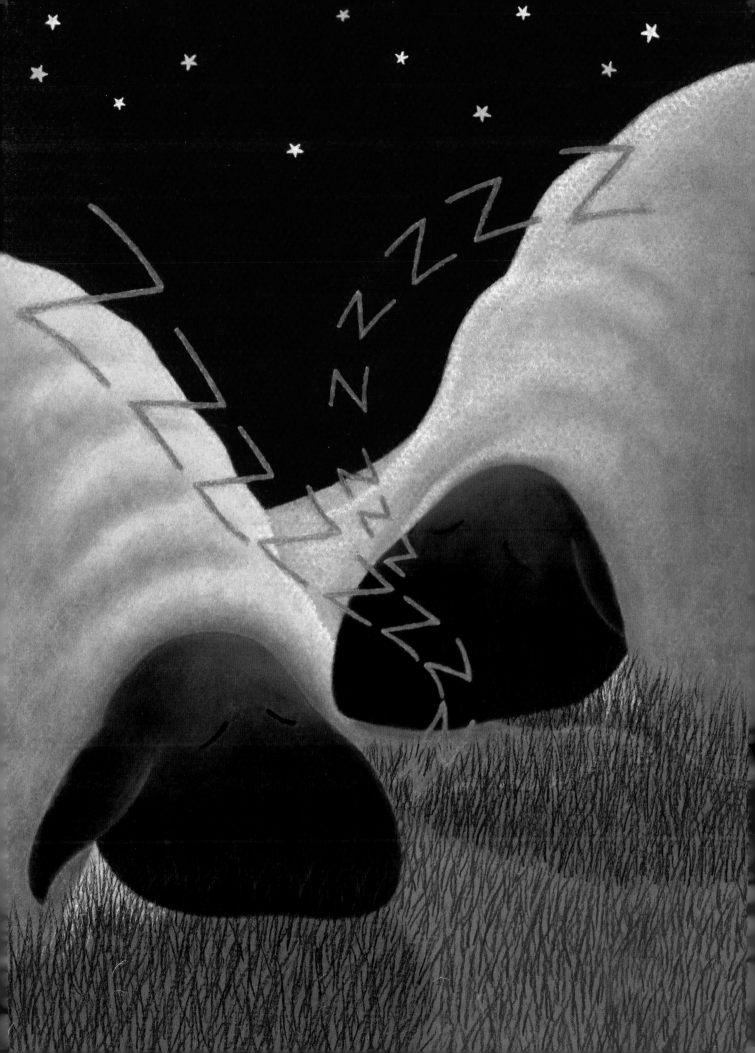

...just like you.
Good night, little lamb.

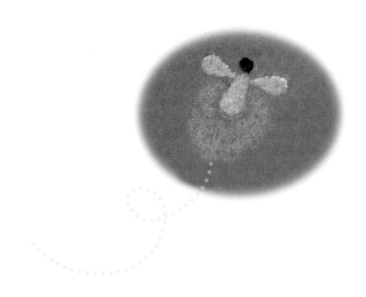